Flairs and Glairs

Publication House

"February- Month of Love"

ISBN No: " 978-93-90799-73-2"
1st Edition
Language – English and Hindi

Flairs and Glairs
Publication House
Regd. Under MSME Act.

Disclaimer

This is a work of fiction and solely represent the thoughts of the corresponding authors of the articles.
Our editors have tried their best to edit the content of all the authors and check the plagiarism.
All the write-ups in this book are unique and are only published in this book.
In case any plagiarism or error is found, only the author is responsible alone, and not the publisher or the Compilers.

Cover Designing and Book Formatting
Shubham Shah and Ishani Agarwal

Acknowledgement

First of all, I thank to the lord Krishna and all other gods & goddess.

I thank here to the Co-authors, who all are the lifeline of this book. Without them, it never completes. All Co-authors are giving their best effort to this book. All I wish for your success in writing.

I would like to be thankful to my parents, friends & family, to support me from first to now. Without there I am unable to do that.

I thank to Anshika Sharma for giving me suggestion for this kind of work. She is always helpful to me. I thank to god for provide me friend, like her, because she always stands with me in every condition.
She always supports me in my all ups and downs.

I am also thankful to the entire team of Flairs & Glairs. Shubham Shah & Ishani Di, support me always from publishers side. Also thanks to Sarvesh upadhyay, who enrich me to the F&G.

About the Book

February: moth of love, this book is all about to various thoughts about love. Across the world we can find love is the most talkative theme. Here our concept totally relatable with the saint valentine.

In February, we can see that love rise across the globe.

Valentine week also scheduled in February.

It is a festival month of lovers from roses to heart & everything.

Emotions of lovers, getting high level in this month.

In this book Co-authors share their own thoughts of love & about the glimpse of February.

All we are having this feel at least one time in entire life. Simply we can talk more & more on this theme. It will be a great book to the readers, who love to read romance genre.

Co Author

Shubham Shah (Founder Flairs and Glairs)
Ishani Agarwal (Co-Founder Flairs and Glairs)

1. Krishan Kant Sen **[Compiler]**
2. Anshika Sharma
3. Nefy
4. Sadhana Nagar
5. Harshit Bansal
6. Priya Kumari
7. Debarati Das
8. Nureen Fatima
9. Nityashree
10. Shreshta Tendulkar
11. Nayanjyoti Baruah
12. R. Amritha Varshini
13. Harini Ganga
14. Nivetha R. C.
15. Trishna Chakraborty
16. S. Suganthi
17. Maryam Ibraheem
18. Keerthana Suriya
19. Pragya Verma
20. Priyanka Pandey
21. Grishma Ninave
22. Mohanapriya K.
23. Kareena Verma
24. Vaisali Pandey
25. Sahina Ghugha
26. Udayan Chetia
27. Ankita Bhatia
28. Jayashree Sahoo

29.	Krishna Motwani
30.	Saumya Bhatia
31.	Machjoke
32.	Devi Shree E. M.
33.	Priyanka Varma
34.	Ka. Parinasri
35.	Falguni Mundhra
36.	Shefali
37.	Yamini Shona Vaishnavi
38.	Sourabh Bhakar
39.	Nesba Sahir
40.	Ms. Ishrat Jahan Noormohammed Khan
41.	Jeevitha S.
42.	Hema Kirthiga J.
43.	Adarsh Kumar Pandey
44.	Kruthigayini K. G.
45.	S. Subhashini
46.	Samia Riaz
47.	Manmita Sarmah
48.	Ankita Sahoo
49.	Suryakanta Biswal
50.	Monika Shanmugam
51.	Vaibhav Gupta

Shubham Shah

(Founder- Flairs and Glairs)

Shubham Shah, an entrepreneur at "Flairs & Glairs" a brand with dynamics in events organizing and cultural educational pan INDIA, is a 26yrs old guy who recently has entered the digital platform of imprinting emotions. He has initiated with his own open mic platform to help budding poets and aspiring writers under his brand named as "Teekhe Zasbaaat"

He is a commerce graduate from the Bhagalpur City of Bihar. He states Writing has impersonated him since childhood and he has now been writing for over a decade!

Cooking, on the other hand, is his passion! He also mentions, trying out new things just tickles him!

When asked sir, Why SPICY EMOTIONS?

He smiled and added, "agar jasbaat teekhe na ho toh wo jasbaat kahan" Spices are all that blends! So do his words!

As a chef, he presents to you his dish! Hot and freshly served! Taste it! Feel it! Enjoy it! You can also find his writing in the Book "Teekhe Zasbaaat" and 50+ Co-authored anthologies. With his passion to explore opportunities across Platforms, he is working with keen devotion and We wish him all the very best for his future ventures.

He is Featured in the **International Magazine De-Mode** for his upcoming solo novel.

He is **Approved by Ne8x for its Lit Fest,** and is a **Golden Star Awards 2020 Winner.**

He is an **India Book of Records Holder** for his Anthology **Satrang,** and has the **Grandmaster** title by **Asia Book of Records**, for the same.

He has also been featured in **Prabhat Khabar, Dainik Jagran** and other renowned Newspaper for his achievements. He has also been awarded with **India Star Republic Award 2021.**

He has been a proud co-author to

India Book of Records (Title- Black)

World Book of Records (Title -15 Wonders of Poetries)

India Book of Records (Title - Aaina)

Vajra World Records Holder (Title - Gustakhi Maaf Hai)

High Range of Records Holder (Title - Gustakhi Maaf Hai)

Share your reviews on his

INSTAGRAM

@spicy_emotions
@shubham4shah
Or via email on
shubham2shah@gmail.com

To stay tuned to his work and opportunities follow his business Handles

INSTAGRAM   FACEBOOK   YOUTUBE

@flairsandglairs
@teekhezasbaaat

WEBSITE:
https://flairsandglairs.in/
https://flairsandglairs.com/

Ishani Agarwal

(Co-Founder- Flairs and Glairs)

Ishani Agarwal hails from the City of Joy, Kolkata.
She is the co-founder of her Community "Teekhe Zasbaaat"
and Flairs and Glairs Publication.
Been a Compiler for 45+ Anthologies, she is in the process for
more. Co-authored in 150+ Anthologies. She is a India Book
of Records Holder, a Vajra World Records Holder, a High
Range of Records Holder and a Bravo Record holder.

Approved by Ne8x for its Lit Fest 2020, and Literary Icon 2020. Also a Golden Star Awards Winner 2020.

She has also been awarded with India Star Republic Award 2021.

She has been featured by the National Magazine "Taree Zameen Par" with the title 'unstoppable'.

Also featured in the International Magazine DeMode for her upcoming solo novel, she is proud to write on social issues, and is happy with the love she is receiving.

Connect with her on Instagram: @Ishani_agarwal_quotes / @compilations_so_far

KRISHAN KANT SEN

A local Boy from Baran Rajasthan, Krishan Kant Sen is a passionate writer. Currently working on his debut Novel. Professional primary teacher likes to work with glorious words. He completed his Master Degree in English from Kota University. His write-ups published in various anthologies in English & Hindi both languages. Mostly works with stories, but sometimes he connects with poetry too. Fictional works is his main need.

He loves to spend time with pen & paper.

He loves to read Novel of Romance genre mostly.

E-mail : krishankant.sen.9@rajasthan.in

Instagram : @krishankant.sen.jr

FEBRUARY MEET

From the Roads of Raipur,
To classic bazaar of Jaipur.
We all have love in the air.
Like a dream without dare.

Emotions becoming high in February.
Seems like fritters try to swim in curry.
She wants to meet me with flurry.
I also wish to meet her in hurry.

Indore was the first destination, we meet.
She amazed me with a specialized greet.
She organized the dates awesome.
Some Hidden surprises were to come.

A diary and pen, she gifted me with love.
My imagination flying high like dove.
She looks beautiful over my thinking.
Sassy eyes having hidden messaging.

Ethnic dress of her stole my heart.
I ordered classy Earrings by Flipkart.
Asking residing address of her home.
She pulled me like a sudden storm.

Eye to eye contact shifted to hesitation.
I pulled back myself like to other nation.
She smiled, I smiled, she ordered food.
We ate food and talking in happy mood.

We turned out from the restaurant.
Wishing to walk some time in Cant.
We went to shopping from mall to mall.
We saw classic Function in Town Hall.

That lovely day was the 4th February.
We met again year after in 12 February.
This time its placing in Fort of Amer.
From there we travelled to Gajner.

Udaipur was the next dream destination.
Abu seemed like our lovely collaboration.
We went Again Indore After these places.
Again reached same restaurant clashes.

We planning to meet again in February.
To recall the memories of love in hurry.
First meet in Indore held by mistake.
Cause I went there for another cake.

She also doesn't know the majestic person.
Whom her family ask to marriage junction
He didn't reach there for some reason.
But we met there without any conclusion.

That was the first meet of unknowns.
Now we are lover by missing worms.

YOU : MY LOVE

Every day I feel you in my feeling.
You are making my heart's dealing.
Hey! My dear, Bring a watch for me.
If not, then please come to me.

Understand my conditions without You.
Can't live here, needs support of you.
I always know, I am not that wants You.
But never imagine life without You.

You are my previous day's report card.
You are my Jet Airways's business class.
You are first class Ticket of Rajdhani Express.
You are queen of my heart's capital delegates.

If we are together, will make New Taj.
If we are together, No need of Topaj.
If we are together, we survive better.
If we are together, sets example later.

Our first meet was in February.
Our last meet was in February.
I write this nonsense in February.
I will marry You in February.

ANSHIKA SHARMA

Anshika sharma, A Lovely girl from Raipur Chhatisgarh, never forget smiling, even in the cringe situations. Life is a motivation in her words. She is beautiful by not only face, even in the honesty also. Her creations look nice in short words, like a drop of ocean with self-motives. Her life reflects many peoples.

She is the founder of "Team Twin Express".

Perfect Love

Sometimes we are not together.
But its less of love, Not Fair.
She loves me so deep.
Without her, I can't beep.
She is the proud of her father.
I am the lifeline of my mother.
Responsibilities handled by her, smoothly.
I don't want to hush her simple life rudely.
We are together or not, doesn't matter.
We will survive for our families better.
Perfect love is not to live life together.
Perfect love asks You to be responsible better.

Nefy

wasted days of petic musings.

And those who were seen dancing were thought insane by those who couldn't hear the music"

Nefy holds these words close to her heart as she lives a life as a stereotypical Indian, stereotypically engineer, stereotypically MBA with a tech job simply doing one atypical thing: Passing her heart a pen. She enjoys writing at the collision of her worlds one of structures and schedules and one of

Bazaar of Love

(I will walk through it myself someday. Maybe to buy, maybe to sell.
I will see excitement as sellers set up their love at dawn, praying for a short day.
I will see nervous flutter as yesterday's scars will be hastily swept away.

Some will open their shops to eager crowds, for fans from far and wide
Some will fly vibrant colors over their tents promising whirlwind romance, young and wild
Some will display their gold, so bold, shimmering in the afternoon's sun, hiding rusted iron underneath the radiance

Some will consider a leniency of bargain to patron's old
Some will whittle their love into appetising molds
Still others will waft spicy aromas in the crisp evening air, urging their love be taken before it is stale and cold

By evening
I will pass some clinking of registers of closed affairs
and excited chatter of near sales
I will also pass those making final pitches for their broken wares

When it is my time, I often wonder,
Will I end my day with a victory cheer
Or like countless others, look to tomorrow for the right compeer)

Until Next Time

(I have decided to
push you away again today
My destiny awaits a warrior uncommitted

Don't call this selfish, merely delayed ecstasy

Because the next time I love you
I will do so when I am ready
And I will do so Unabashed, Unapologetic, Irredeemable

I will give you my all
I will free fall into you
Into what you do to my life
And take the path at the fork
That I brushed past for another

Will you be there for me?

I promise that I will remember
to Fall in love with you
Over and Over
When I'm ready)

SADHNA NAGAR

She is Sadhana nagar from Baran Rajasthan. She has completed her bachelor in IT. She is crazy about her dreams. She loves to write & always wants to learn more new things. She is a girl, who lives her life with whole heart and freedom.

February

February, A month with unlimited feeling.
February, A month with lovable sealing.

February, Having Valentines desire of love.
As like, in love, Ant rescue life of the Dove.

February, Chocolaty month of the year.
New couple's love air in top of the gear.

February, A month smoothy like teddy.
Looks alike love speaks Clary shady.

Promise of lovers stand like magical curry.
Fluppy blessing to love fame in February.

All pleasure, that all lovers want to get.
February makes their love to celebrate.

Crispy food sassy cake and lovely kiss.
February is the month, All lovers miss.

New shop runs near the park of Valentine.
Not the Herby, but all pains removed mine.

Heroics Rose, milky cake and French kiss.
February deals lovers to make them bliss.

HARSHIT BANSAL

He is Harshit bansal from Baran rajasthan. He is an Engineer by Education.

An old school Boy living in this modern Era, still find Pen & Paper more comfortable than the Mobile Keyboard.

Passionate about cycling, as always up for swimming.

Lovely month February

After the glossy and cool month January.
We all are facing Lovely month February.

All the year, we are in love with regularity.
In February, we getting love with specialty.
Can't pack this in any limited super age.
All are waiting this with their entity gaze.
As it has the classy Love Valentine week.
All the Admirers having feelings at peak.

Newly Lovers excite to their imagination.
Oldies grades express by communication.
Something new, something old tradition.
But all believe this with their superstition.

Roses bells rhyming, chocolates singing.
Gifts call changing, Cake shines pudding.
To their enthusiastic love, they are hugging.
Express feelings through lovely greeting.

Decor things by bright stickers and fury.
We all waiting for lovely month February.

Priya Kumari

I am student cum rising poet from Muzaffarpur Bihar. Want to be a romantic poet.
My passion is all about writing and my writing is all about love.

Love and Its manifestation

If missing you is madness
and this madness is love
then I want to be mad forever.

If texting, you repeatedly is loss of self-respect
and this loss of self-respect is love
then I want to lose self-respect every time.

If waking up for you till morning is foolishness
and this foolishness is love
then I want to be fool till my last breath.

If waiting for you is waste of time
and this waste of time is love
then I want to waste my time whole life.

If thinking of you is obsession
and being obsessed is love
then I want to be obsessed for always.

If writing about you is my passion
and this passion is love
then I want to be passionate for lifetime.

If loving you, is weakness
and this weakness is love
then I want to be weak more and more.

The Sweetest Gift

Thanks love for the sweetest gift,
You returned with the biggest rift.
After so many months and years,
We met and celebrated with beers.
I saw, Flashing call on your phone,
Number was saved with "my own".
I just ignored believing blindly in you,
You were looking gorgeous in blue.

One day you called me to meet soon,
I became very happy thinking it boon.
But where my smile had gone when,
You decided to break up. After then,
You went and blocked my number,
I tried to contact you but you were
gone already too much far from me.
Thanks love, for gifting this to me.

Debarati Das

She strongly believes that one should never settle for something less than what one deserves and with this belief, she has come forward to be a part of this anthology.

She hopes that she will be getting all of our heartiest love and support throughout her journey.

Her write-ups have been published in more than 100 national and international anthologies. She is really honoured to be a part of this anthology and would like to extend her thanks of gratitude to all the members of this anthology and the readers as well.

One less lonely night

The stars over us kept shining so bright,
Looking at someone special gave me great delight,
The unspoken words in those eyes kept me standing upright,
We both proved to be in love at first sight.
The sudden gasp of wind touched me as a whole with immense pleasure,
Your presence felt to me more than an inexhaustible treasure.
One step by one step we came closer,
Our inner feelings got a stupendous exposure.
When you started invoking me to be highly versatile,
Somehow I started getting hypnotized by your affectionate smile.
We broke all the boundaries in love according to stereotypes,
Our utmost concern for each other was enough for our sorrow to get completely wiped.
It has been two years since we parted happily with each other,
Since then my heart has always convinced me to accept you as my elder brother.

Nureen Fatima

She believes in hard work
She sincerely does her task

Courageous and ambitious

Love

My life would have been nothing without you....
You always give me most beautiful things...
Always there to help me in any way,
The loving things you have done for me,
I could never repay....
I Love You Mom
You always lift me up
When I was down
Keep me humble,
And love me no matter what happens...
You are like a star in my life,
Keep shining always no matter what happens....
You are flawless Mom
I want to be like you....

I LOVE YOU MOM

Nityashree

Payal Kamdi from Maharashtra.
Penning her thoughts by penname Nityashree.
A girl with passion in writing mess with the heart and mind. The picking of ink and fell down of paper which comes along shadow. Belives writing helps to concrete thoughts and manifest faster.

Love

Before I met you,
I didn't know if love existed
before you came in my life
and honestly quite twisted.
I pushed everyone away
and kept myself apart.
Silence engulfed me
every time talked about love.
It's amazing when you touch me
feeling in depth connection.
You brought sunshine
when I only saw rain.
You brought joy
when I was only sad.
Every thought from yours
fills me with sweet emotions.
My fondest gets fulfil
My life dream gets verified.
Your masculinity attracts me
your silence shivers me.
I wrap myself in your warmth
Rainbow arrive in my life.
I thank God you be in my life
And I thank you for everything.

I adore you

You will never know my love
You will never know the depth of missing you.
Each moment it feels like so blue.
When someone talks about you
I have tears in my eyes
I know that I may sound so kiddish
But I don't want to be so wise
Coz there is no purpose living without you
I can't tell you that you are a apart
You stay in my mind
and my heart
I pray that you never leave me alone
You are my life's comfort zone.
I miss all the moments spent with you.
When you arrive with bunch of flowers
My hearts fell down in your soul.
I even don't know how to express
I just came closer you and wrap you in my world.
I kept thanking you are in my life.
My devotion is you and love is you and my happiness lies in
you.

Shreshta Tendulkar

It's alright if you are not a part of the pack. It takes courage, conviction and a bold step to stand as a lone wolf. And that one step began my journey of writing.

THE STAY

He sat at the table
Watched the snow fall
He was alone he was lonely
The empty chair said it all
He drank his tea, it was stale and cold
But it tasted better than his life
Which had become a dead pursuit of a love untold.
He stood there he looked alive
But his heart was beating somewhere far away.
He believed she would come
And all that was destined for him was a stay.
"My love will come" he said
Bring back the life of my soul
Put back the broken pieces of my heart
And make my life once again whole.
Hoping to see her and be with her
Is what he desired to come true
Maybe tomorrow definitely tomorrow
He would live his dream of telling her "I love you ".
He never gave up on dreaming
He persisted because he just knew
A wait for true love is worth waiting
And it's a blessing only to a few.
Even though they were miles apart.
Her thought never left his heart.
He loved her then. He loved her now.
It's always when and never how.

Why did I

Why did I feel my heart?
When I first heard your voice
There was care and love with no lies and bluff
I believed I was deaf and that no soul could speak concern
But your warmth bought me home and it was before you that
I surrendered
You were never in my past, you are too true to be in the
future but it's in my thoughts that you reside and that is
where my heart lies
Your soul reveals itself whenever I find myself in trouble
And it is before you that I bow......
 timid and humble
I wish I could explain your eyes and how the sound of you
gives me butterflies
How you make me complete and that you belong to heaven
for angels to greet.

Nayanjyoti Baruah

He's Nayanjyoti Baruah,a poet, essayist and a translator, pursuing M. A. in English Literature from Gauhati University, Assam, India. He has written about 150 poems. His poems have been appeared in Tayls, Rasa Literary Review, Felicity, Akhore, Meghali Budhidrom, The Fiction Project, A Too Powerful Word, Necro Magazine etc. He's the Co-author of the Bag of Knowledge. Being an Indian Teenager, Shining Dreams and Together Forever (these three will be published in 2021). Several of his poems will be published in two anthologies, Heart Beats and Third Eye Butterfly in 2021, in USA. He's written two essays and five short stories. Currently He's writing his first novella. He's 22 years old.

Because We Love

If someone asks you,
Let him or her know that
You have someone
Whom you love more than love.

If someone asks you,
Why do you love him more than love?
Let him or her know that
Because he loves you more than love.

If someone asks you
Why does he love you more than love?
Let him or her know that
Because you're his sunlight and moonlight,
Because you're his home
Where he wanted to dwell,
Because you're his destination
Where he wanted to go,
Because he sees you while dreaming,
Because he sees you when he wakes up.

If someone asks you
Why do you trust him?
Let him or her know that
Because our love is love, which is
Beyond anyone's suspicious love.

Love Never Dies

I'm trying to forget you Sweetheart
Every day, every moment.
Sometimes I go to the liquor store
And drink more,
But only the senses fall asleep,
You have always been awake in my sense.
Sometimes I look at other girls,
Maybe they are beautiful,
But your naked face is visible in them.
They become bitter to me.
Sometimes I write a poem at 12 o'clock,
But your presence is in every line.

What I do?
How can I ignore you?
When will I forget you?
How will I get rid of you?

Because of you, my Sweetheart
I can't sleep well
I don't feel better tonight and every night
After you leave, sweetheart.

I haven't forgotten you yet.
But why?

R. Amirtha varshini

Amirtha varshini was born in Tirunelveli. She is a girl who is trying to make all her dreams come true. Writing is her passion. She loves spending time with books. In short, books are the world to her. She writes a lot about social issues. Her writings will be continued.

A reprise of life:

Bonded by trust
Cover our crust
Maybe at first sight
or by time's fate
Dig the live soul
Snatch the unique Throne
Sweet flavour
Want to inhale every moment
Sprays the hearty breeze
Sings mourn to woe
Cover as eyelid
Clutch in-between arms
When we need aid
Give its lap to bow
Around us like a warm
Wander like as a pinky foot
Became charmed when getting it
Take us to walk up to last.

A. Harini Ganga

Harini Ganga was born in Nellai and pursuing her college studies in Coimbatore. Writing is her habit, hobby, passion, and love from her childhood. Between reality and fantasy, she writes her thoughts.

Indubitably, It's a miracle

The bliss that is showered on
Unlocks the heart and read
Put on efforts to be happy
Knows the magic of melting anger
North star of life
Gifts worth keeping memories
Makes to wait with bells on
Promising truth in the ambitious world
Cherish each other's dream
Make feel what tenderness is
Doesn't falls for the beauty
Mesmerizes in soulful words
Wishes to be together
Even in names
Enjoys silly talks
Values thoughts
Feels glee every time
Fly in the air
With delicate wings.

Nivetha R C

Nivetha R C, a young poetess from Coimbatore, Tamil Nadu. She graduated BA English Literature from PSGR Krishnammal College for Women. Currently, she is pursuing MA English in KSG College of Arts and Science, Coimbatore. She started writing poems from the age of 13. She used to write in Tamil and English.

Nivetha likes to personify the things around her and tries to reveal its emotions through her words.

She is interested to deliver the unheard conversations between two non-living things. She likes to write poems with rhyming words. Sometimes she uses to write acrostic poems too.

Colourful Roses

"Hey, buddy. Look at our seller's face.
'Today it is so crowded in his place'
Do you know any specific reason?
'Yes. I think it is the love season.'
Oh, buddy, do you think that February arrived?
'Yes, I think so even this circumstance can describe.'
Haha look at the boy he is admiring our friends
'This is a special day to buy us he spends'
Can you guess which colour he will choose?
'Of course Red there is no excuse'
Why can't they choose others any reason for their refusal?
'They think red is best for their love proposal'
Our seller will have profit today
'For that only he came here without delay'
These boys compare their loved ones to Rose
'They think that comparison helps when they propose'
Look at the roses of white
'They have become so quite'
See the roses in yellow
'They have kept below'
Red roses are bidding byes to their friends
'Because they know that their bond ends'
So today's star performer is the red team
'For Valentine's day red is the main theme'
Hey that boy is looking at our basket
'He is even taking money from his jacket'

Maybe it's time for us to bid farewell to each
'Separation is the lesson what our life teach.' "
Wind heard this conversation of two red roses
After their separation, it starts itself to disposes

Trishna Chakraborty

Trishna Chakraborty is a writer from Dimahasao, Assam.she is a student of English Literature. She writes poetry, Quotes and micro tale stories. She is a coauthor of 20+Anthologies and a compiler. She is the founder of @ink_your_words and she wants to be a famous writer.

Let's be closer

Beneath the sky
In the moonlight,
Like the stars are in infinite numbers,
My love for you is enormous.
Staring at me while coming closer
Stars are shining as we are.
I feel your breathe.
Holding my waist and thrusting me on the sack.
Loving me like there is no next day,
In the dark we can see our love grow.
My craving for your touch.
Is wild as we are.
Playing with your hair, my lips got tacky and dry
I wet myself with u.

Yearn for thee

I met you it's my destiny
In a distance you are, but I feel the beat of your heart.
The care you show to me
I can see the love in your eyes,
You are a wrecked one all said
But I found my complete soul in you,
Each time, I want to make you know
How much I miss you,
You always catches my smile and
Promised me my eyes will never be in tears...
I don't know where my ways will go
But I wanna walk by holding your hands
The rest of my life I wanna be in your arms.

S.Suganthi

Suganthi has been writing for over two years. She provides philosophical writings. Her educational background in English literature has given her a broad base for writings. Her books are available in Amazon kindle named Heartly Sayings and Healing journey-1.

The love breathing

The love breathing
between two of us,
is unexplainable,
if it is explainable,
I'm sure my nervous
& happy heart
couldn't convey it.
Like all other people,
I had a desire of
having a prince.
And I'm more than lucky
to have you as mine.
Like a fairytale,
you don't come
to save me every time
Because you know
I can do that for myself.
But you make me realize
the strength that a princess
needs to save herself.

Our chemistry is as precious
as a constellation of stars,
and the fervour of your love
keeps my heart warm
which once froze by
the coldness of the world.
Love comes in
unexpected ways
like a sudden wave.
It reaches you when
you stop searching for it.
It comes to you
when you first,
learn to find it within.
It comes when you fall
for the life you have.
It comes when you
don't blame it
because of the lover
who couldn't love you.

Maryam Ibraheem

She is a realist yet likes spontaneity
Loves to look at things from their underlying factors and high view point
Believes we are all intertwined and interconnected.

TALES FROM THE HEART

I used to think, how could I talk about love when my heart still aches from your departure?
How could I sing along with the birds when all that's left in me are hums of sorrow?
How do I smile joyfully when my heart threatens to elope in search of you?

I thought we could make a story like the fairy tales,
But here I lay with feelings neither in black, white nor grey.
 lost somewhere in the clutters of colors and presence of nay.

How do I begin our story that's turned out to be mine only?
How do I conclude singly what we began together?
How do I write that we'll never meet again?

One thing I know, some feelings come to awaken the love that's laid dormant within us.
They act as the water and sunlight we need to sprout forth.
They unlock the box of nutrients hidden in the deepest Chambers to nourish our withered souls.

For love is too much to exist in one person only.
Love is cosmopolitan,
Love is in all that breathes and all that lives,
Love has always been and will always be the sustaining force of the multiverse.

Facets of love

What then is love?
It's more than the butterflies that collide in your tummy when you sight your beloved.
It's not a feeling that engulfs you and leave you hanging.
It doesn't promise yay and do nay.

Love is the look of concern from the medics when they can't guarantee your survival of a surgery.
It's the horror on the faces of the emergency team when you're stuck in the rubbles.
It's the sudden strength in the firefighters' legs when they jump in to trade their lives with yours.

Love is why we haven't killed each other with our atomic bombs and nuclear weapons.
It's why we strive to fight hunger
And why we struggle against racism, imperialism, fascism, anti-feminism and all the isms that are inhumane.
Love is unicorn, multi skilled and multi coloured,
Love is Lion, brave and strong,
Love is snake, slythering and winding,
Love is falcon, wild and high.

Love is Phoenix, it'll always rise from the ashes,
It's drops healing and mending our souls.
Let the Phoenix of love fly aboard and heal the world.

Keerthana Suriya

She is Ms.KEERTHANA SURIYA a highly aspired, dynamic medical student, social-worker, a passionate writer and classical dancer who is engaging in self and social development, building relationships and exhibiting integrity. She is Co-Author of various other anthologies.

She is Founder of WACHC Foundation - Women And Children Health Care and also holding the position of Women's Health Empowerment Project Head in the trust Women's Renaissance Centre. She strongly believes that "When women and children rise, their communities and countries rise with them".

Follow her on Instagram - @keethusm

I WANT TO BE YOUR ONE AND ONLY

Dear Beloved,

I found someone, a truly beautiful soul
with whom I can have a conversation
of anything and everything.
He is someone who gives me all freedom to speak without
any terms and conditions.
He explores the world with me
He is someone with whom I can have
endless fun and at the same time
he is someone who shows me
the right and best path,
makes me believe in myself,
makes me think in different perspectives,
helps me overcome my fears, and helps me
to learn and understand about life.
He is someone who always says
I'm his favourite.

Yes! That someone is YOU
You are truly a beautiful soul
and an amazing person
Your presence, your words,
your love, care and support
makes me feel complete.
I am so lost in loving you that
I can never separate my soul from yours.
If this is not called true love,
I don't know what else is!
I don't want to be your favourite,
I want to be your one and only.

Lots of Love,
Keethu

Pragya Verma

Pragya Verma hails from Prayagraj, Uttar Pradesh. She is a poetess and a writer. She has done 80+ anthologies, and two international anthologies and currently doing two world record anthologies as a co-author. She is also compiling two anthologies named, "Shades Of Night", "In A Relationship With Success". She has a great interest in making paintings and doing photography. She loves to gain spiritual knowledge and tries to find peace everywhere. You can follow her on Instagram: @wordsofpragya

Mine Forever

He has a love in his eyes,
In which, all my happiness lies.
With him there's no scary nights,
Every moment feels delight.

He is as calm as river,
With whom I can live forever.
His smile is like a rainbow,
That takes away my sorrow.

The peace I get with him,
That couldn't be found at the rim.
Nightmares don't scare me now,
As he stays with me anyhow.

I feel calmness of river in his love,
His love makes me shine brighter than the stars above.
He brought light in my dark life,
From my heart, he had removed all the strife.

I want his love forever and ever,
Oh lord, just make this man mine forever.

Those fallen eyes of mine

Those fallen eyes of mine,
Wants to take all your pain,
Make you feel so fine,
And happy once again.
Don't let our love to die,
Baby, you don't have to cry,
Don't worry! I won't say any lie,
Cause i hate saying goodbye.
I'm always there for you,
Just smile and get used to.
New memories are waiting for us,
And all I need is your love and trust.

Priyanka Pandey

Priyanka is a banker by profession, but her heart lies in writing, she finds her solace in writing, she says "to write is to meditate".

Flames of love

The flames of her love was flickering rapidly.
With doubts on his coming, still she was waiting eagerly.
Typing and deleting messages on phone for him anxiously.
And then the thought lingered in her mind abruptly.
What if he never comes, and she has to be alone Perpetually.
And then a beep with flashing light on her phone suddenly.
The beats of her heart just increased multiply.
"I am here, open the door", and she was thrilled now badly.
She opened the door and smiled at him severely.
But then she was shocked, and amazed equally.
He was there on his knees with a bunch of rose and said softly,
"Will you be mine my princess, and be a part of my family?"
Now this was the moment she had been waiting ardently.
Down she went on her knees, as she could speak barely.
The flickering flame of love, now calmed yet rose higher passionately.

Lovelorn

Those greys of her hair, the wrinkle of her eyes, Her pale body, and dim eyes.

Those collar bones like a thin branch of a dead tree peeped out, as no flesh was left, where it could hide.

Spoke of her end days, and depicted that it was time for a good bye.

She raised her finger and pointed the wall, there was a picture of her dressed up as a bride.

She had a last gaze on it and a deep exhale, that was her last moment and then she died.

I looked at the picture, which had no groom in it, and opened the diary kept on her head side.

She was a lady, left by a man that too on the day of her marriage, which never materialised.

She never went for marriage, nor could love anyone and stayed love deprived.

I don't know whom to blame?? The man or herself? for her lovelorn life.

Grishma Ninave

Grishma Ninave was born and brought up in the Orange City, Nagpur. She is a Science graduate and an avid reader. Thriller is her favourite genre. Currently working as, a Project Head at Flairs & Glairs Publication House. A firm believer that happiness is not something that you find, it's something that you create. She loves travelling, blogging and listening to music.

Mountains' Story

The mountains told me a story
Of their love with the clouds,
Of desires every rain brought along
And the kisses they had shared...

The mountains told me a story
Of their affinity with the heights,
Of the dreams of rising above
And the thrill they'd brought...

The mountains told me a story
Of their relationship with the trees,
Of the birds that harbored them
And the delight they creates...

Hangover

The hangover of when I last met you
still ponders over my head.
Where the eyes were grave
but still conveyed what they were not meant to...

The Hangover of when I last met you
is like a thunderstorm I wish to get rid of.
Where so less was spoken
but so much was said...

The hangover of when I last met you
Confuses me like a jigsaw puzzle.
Where the eyes seem to smile
and the lips seem to cry...

The hangover of when I last met you
is like the red sky.
Where the Sun loses its existence
only to give way to the moon....

Mohanapriya.K

Co-author Mohanapriya.K is a good writer from Tamilnadu, India. She has completed her Bachelor's degree in Engineering stream. She has been a writer for one year as her passion. She wants to be a best compiler and curator in future. Yet she sincerely hope that this writing journey of her will bring her many successes. She also loves singing.

February 14 - Valentine's day

February is a month of love.
we are celebrating Valentine's day on February 14.
There is no limit to true love and there is no rule for unconditional love.
The privilege of our life is to live with the person with whom we desire to live and to spend our entire life with him.
The love we show to others should be our own volition and we should not allow others to interfere too much in that desire.
We should not expect the same love that we pay to be forced on us by the person we love.
Maybe if we look forward to doing so sometimes only one disappointment overwhelms us.
The most important thing is to live with love in love and if you forget it then that love will be gone.

Want to live with my love

We will spend our precious time with the people we love the most.
We will give unconditional love and live happily.
What a beautiful feeling love is!
Love wins or loses but it is always filled with a feeling of beauty in the mind.
Because lovers can lose but love never fails.
Provides the ability and strength to accomplish anything.
The love that offers such ability is the highest!
Allurement is a blessing for someone. An antidote for pain.
The effect of the drug is so great.
How can such a big thing be taken lightly.
Two hearts are one heart!
Then how to make one into two hearts.

Kareena verma

She is a computer science student currently pursuing the Bachelor of Computer application, she has been writing since one year and a co-author of many Anthology and when she is usually alone, has deep relation with her pen and diary. She is very introvert girl with full of optimistic soul and an ambitious girl. A teenage girl filled with millions dreams of thoughtful brain, in this world only her pen & diary is the best friend to penned her pain in the blank pages of life Diary.

And same as her name Kareena delineate alike her name, sanguine with her soul, pure with her heart, innocent with her straightforward thoughtful perceptions!

Love Vibes

Whenever I meet you, to talk with you
I just lost myself forever in you
Those 1 am talk with you,
My silliness questions & your sweet answers
Hehe! How do I always bore you with it?
"Do you ever cry?", Yes as usual, always
"You said to me with shyness"
I always asking to myself,
"How do we both feel to each other?"
Without saying any words
"How do we understand to each other with just text formats?"
I don't know, why those weird feelings happened with us?
Sometimes I thought, I'm disturbing you,
"I don't wanna disturb you" with my words,
I don't wanna hurt you ever with my words,
I don't wanna lose you ever, to lost myself again
And "if someone ask to me"
What did you get best ever in this year?
" I'll tell your name just only my friend"
Thank you to being my soulmate of my every tearful pains!

Why are you always nice with me?

Why do you make me so much special everyday with more care of mine!
How do you feel my pain; when I'm really not okay; but I'm replying you in the text " that I'm fine, please don't worry at all"; Why I'm so Possessiveness about you;
"Am I really fall in love with you?"
When you talk to me,
When you share your favourite songs with me and how is turn into my favourite too; when I meet you in my dreams always;
When you hold my hands; Kiss me on my forehead,
You came across to touch my neck; When I'm really in Deep pain, frustrated
You just hold me in your shoulders
How you hug me tightly; then I forget everything in you; please don't left me hold me tight in arms; You came in me as blooming flower in winter; Let's just listen our both fav song in headphones!
With one cup coffee with you!

Vaisali Pandey

A college student on the path of getting a degree to achieve her dreams and goals. Also, a rising poet doing her best to relate with people's emotions, while trying to cope up with every hurdles in her life.

Love blooms

Right In My Arms
I wait for these night's
Silent and silent by the gray moon
To take a look at you,
As we went out by the moonlight.

I cannot keep my excitement in bay,
If it shall clasp this star in your wing!
Your breath like the bubble of a play,
Set a proud spirit on our love!

Without thy love this hope has known
Now my life's a new winter of desire
The cold winds and warm rays,
Bathes our skin with our love.

There shall be no distance between us,
From now on let's hold each other,
For few more hours, maybe till-
The sun rises and birds chirps joyfully.

Let's go and break away all the chains,
Let's not listen to those unnecessary voices,
Know for it after the wood in rain,
Or not a breeze will do if it ran.

Let's just focus on us, will ye?
Why will I wait for their permission?
They will take you away from me,
But this time I might be greedy for myself.

I will sweep ye off your feet,
Keep you from the fire of fire,
I will let no one harm you,
My love for you will protect you.

You are looking astonishing in a white dress,
Standing adored from your electric light,
Eyes filled with youth,
I see a moment before your sight.

I see myself in your enchanting eyes,
Lighting my heart with something of gold,
Glowing fiercely in my body,
Running wildly in my blood.

The need to hold you in my arms,
To feel yourself let go of all the vile things,
Which is seperating yourself from me,
My love I am as harmless as a butterfly.

So let go of those chains,
Come running away in my arms,
I will hold your body and heal all your injuries,
Leaving only the scars and loving them altogether.

Sahina Ghugha

Sahina Ghugha is 20-year-old b.com student at Saurashtra university Rajkot. She is from Jamnagar city of Gujarat. She is state level winner in poetry competition 2017. She is Co-author of 10+ anthologies. She is an amazing writer and poet and she wants do something for society through her pen.

Insta ID: - Itz_Sahina_write

Love spirit

Lotus blooms in the pond like your smile
 I am lost only after seeing you
 When I get my eyes on you, I start dreaming
 In reality, there is no scope for us to be one
 But what to do with this heart that starts beating your smile
 Does not understand that this heart depends only on you
 Everything stops when your voice resonates in my ears
 There are millions of beautiful faces, but this heart is relieved
just by your smile
 I will not be able to meet you but my love is just you and it
will never be less.
 Because I have loved your spirit, which will remain intact.

Rainbow

When I saw a rainbow,
I am Like rain drops,
 Saw you in the sun
 When I saw a garden,
I settled in the form of oysters,
I saw you in a deer.

When I saw a river,
I jump like waves,
I saw you in the edges.
When I saw one night,
I shine in your light,
I saw you in the stars.

Udayan Chetia

Udayan Chetia was born on September 26, 2003 into a middle class family from Dhemaji district, Assam. He also known by his nickname "Ron". He started writing poems, quotes, short-stories etc.; when he was in 6th standard in English, Hindi and Assamese languages. Udayan pursued his HSLC Exam from Vivekananda Kendra Vidyalaya, Dhemaji in the year 2019 and currently studying at Crescent Academy, Jorhat. His most of the writings were published on his school magazine "Jnanam". He was inspired by his father for writing as his father himself is a writer.

Love

Love,
It is an intense feeling of
deep affection or,
a great interest and pleasure
in something.

It can be animals, human beings,
or,
it can be some other things
 in which,
we feel a deep affection.

It is love,
Who teaches us to
live, respect, trust, honesty
and many more.

A love is the emotion
shared between a couple who has been
married or still passionate
about each other.

Ankita Bhatia

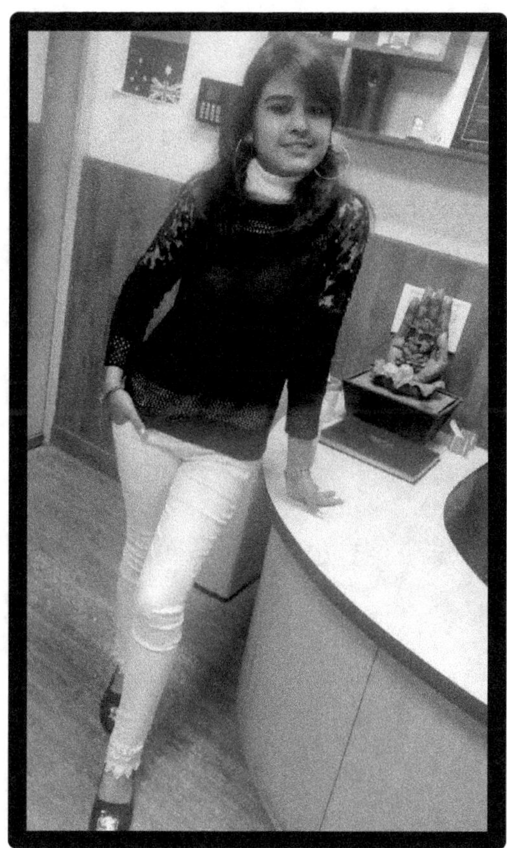

A girl hailing from New Delhi pursuing B.SC second year and working as Immigration Consultant in real world and entrepreneur in virtual world. An influencer and a blogger.

Happy Valentine's Day to my love

My love?!!
Yes, my love,
No……
No please don't confuse with the word "boyfriend."
I'm talking about that valentine of mine who is with me since
d day I start taking breadth, and that valentine who will never
leave me till my last breadth.

I'm talking about that man who is every girl's first love
"A father".

Father is such a man who never ditch her girl, who fulfils all
her wishes without any conditions and loves his daughter
unconditionally.
and yes I have such a valentine and no one can ever replace a
dad's love...
Happy Valentine's day daddy thanks for everything.

Jayashree Sahoo

Jayashree Sahoo is habitant of ODISHA.

Her writings started on yourquote,notojo and mirakee like writing platforms. You can search her on yourquote by name of Jaya Jayashree. Nowadays She is member of many writing communities and earned a lots of certificates through her writings.

She is Co-author of 170+ anthologies. Also She is Compiler of many anthologies in Hindi, English and Odia languages. Currently She is working as project head and board member of a reputed publication.

According to her, if you don't express your inner feelings towards someone, then just write those on a paper and making yourself happy for without reason.

Also she has interested in singing, travelling, photography also. Among of these extra activities She studying Nursing on Govt. medical and she has an aim for be a RN nurse and good writer.

Insta id -@mixing_of_emotions

Email.id- jayashreesahoo665@gmail.com

Without you

After that incident,
you left out,
Then I feel alone
I'm feeling like,

have body without shadow
have life without heart
have everything without nothing
have a face without smile

have a desire without mood
Still I'm waiting, for you eagerly,
Because I always love you,
And I'll do love to only you,

Though, your memory reminds me
 in every minute,
But, I ignore that from my mind, but
not from my heart,
All your love, always remember that
You are always with me

But it's not in reality,
It's just a fantasy,
Someone said, love is endless,
And that I feel in days,

Krishna Motwani

@unique__blog_

Krishna Motwani is a Student currently.
She uses to pen down her feelings.
She is a moody girl.
She started writing in the month of june,2020.
She writes in her free time.
She writes some motivational quotes or poetries too and practices artworks also.
She lives her life like a bird
As bird flies freely and enjoys life like that she also lives her life freely and enjoy fullest.
For motivating and inspiring poems and quotes, you can check her on Instagram :

My Love: My smile!

It was the day when I seen you first time and got a smile,
It was a stranger meet while.

We were unknown to each other,
Now promised to be with each other for ever.

I can't see, in your eyes tears,
For losing you I always fears.

You are the one who refreshes me,
Makes surprises, I always see.

You are my will power,
Be always my life's book cover.

Just can't express my feelings in words,
I know how much you loves.

Always takes care,
Says that I am rare.

My heart will love you forever,
Can't forget our memories ever.

The one whom I love unconditionally is only you,
I just can't live without you.

Take me away with you with happiness,
Let's leave all of our sadness.

Saumya Bhatia

Saumya Bhatia is a 21-year-old, Delhi girl. She is currently pursuing her post-graduation. She started writing as a hobby and now this hobby is slowly and gradually developing into passion. She aspires to be a writer and want to reach to people's heart through her writing.

'Love'

Love is pure,
Like a Dove you allure,
Love is deep,
Like the water in the reep,
Love is beautiful,
Like the Cukko bird sitting on the roof,
Love is warming,
Like the sizzling wood with the fire,
Love is affectionate,
Like a mother patting the child,
Love is caring,
Like a sister handling her little one,
Love is amorous,
Like it is away from all the rumours,
Love is what,
What everyone believes it.

'Love Stages'

The themed stages of alluring love,
Making the people aware about this word,
It first just starts with 'attraction'
As one came into your life,
As a distraction,
The second it comes to infatuation,
As someone sitting in front of you,
As an admiration,
The third it reaches to love,
As someone blossoming into your life,
As a pure white dove,
The fourth comes to trust,
You both started believing that what is must,
The fifth we are on the grounds of worship,
Where you believe that everything is around this relationship,
The sixth we are at the verge of madness,
Where we feel there is no room for sadness,
Finally, we end with death,
Making all of us believe that your love was my breath.

MachJoke

MachJoke is an upcoming writer from Chennai, capital of TamilNadu. He's like a mad guy to write madly words, but creates a path of emotions to connect directly the readers. He's an undergraduate mathematician and also tuition master. He has been writing the quotes and poetry for last 8 months as a passion. His ambition to become a good writer for his future.

My Love - I Surrendered You

Remember...!
The cupid has strike my heart by his bow,
To Fall in love with you at sweet flow.
I Keenly to see you without removing my eyes that day,
Lived in the world of fairy tale like the flies.

Flying in my dreams to be cross the limit of sky,
Start to loving with each other by soulfully,
By each and every single moment at happily.
The love can be healed our combined heart,
Without the distance to separate from apart.

Over the days, the love has been so strong,
No one can break out the filthy bond.
Eyes to eyes, heart to heart, in wonder,
Fully myself to be in with you at surrender.!
Hold your hands and live like forever.!

Love Has No Boundaries

My Dear Sweetheart,
There's no limit for my love that I could showing you,
Everyday my love has been growing up,
Like the rate of miscellaneous in our state,
I don't know the exact or accurate or approximate,
But I'll know that how much I loved you in my life,

Days are gone, years are reborn, by
Watching my love to being exists at infinity;
Either I'll be with you or you'll be with me,
Both of them have mixed and mingled at single heart,
There's no one can live without love in our creature,

One day it could be reaching the end of the sky,
For sharing my love to you like the tremendous hazards,
Because I realized my life to nobody can show to me;
After I got you in my life of destiny with love,
It's like an abide of happiness in my life forever.!

Devi Shree E.M

Devi Shree, being ambitios, standing under Tamil-Nadu roof!
"make thing happen!" says this girl with a lot of courage!...
She was broken, but waken by her goals!

Physic researcher.

Poet's Love!

He was my secret page!
His love is my poetry!
His kisses are my metaphor!
His hugs are my repetition!
His cuddles are my Anaphora!
His Nights were my Personification!
I am his Wordsworth and he is my "My Heart Leeps up!"

Love was beyond heart!

With all stress in India!
My heart stayed at Paris!
With loads of love!
With loads of tears!
Beyond families!
Beyond countries!
He, with my memories, there!
I, with his love here!
Video calls were lenghthy!
Phone call were, for hours!
Love was beyond heart!
Beyound my boundries!

Priyanka Varma

She is Priyanka Varma studying Masters of Pharmacy from Visakhapatnam. She is a National and Central Zonal Sports Player along with being a Classical Dancer and an Artist. Along with these, she is also a poetess fond of writing her thoughts.
she believes that "The best and most beautiful things in this world cannot be seen or even heard, but must be felt with the heart. Life without love is like a tree without blossoms or fruit".

MY VALENTINE

At first I wasn't looking for love.
I wanted no one in my life,
for I had totally given up.

But for just a moment
I gave you a chance.
I let my guard down,
One last try I thought.

I never imagined that I
would find all this and more.
The best friend and lover
that one could ever hope for.

A friend I can count on,
to listen and understand.
A lover for me to hold
who is truly a good man.

I love when you smile
and all the things you do,
so I want you to know that
you're my dream come true.

I know in my heart now
that no one else will do.
Happy Valentine's Day, Baby!

PROMISE

If you were my world, then I'd be your moon,
your silent protector, a night-light in the gloom.
Hold me tight to your heart
And promise me that we will never be apart.
Promise me that your heart will always beat for me.
If you were my island, then I'd be your sea,
caressing your shores, soft and gentle I'd be.
My tidal embrace would leave gifts on your sands,
but by current and storm, I'd ward your gentle lands.
Each word you say makes me love you more.
Nothing will ever stop my love for you, you are my soul.
Night and day, day and night, I want to be by your side.
Every moment of every day you are always on my mind.
So in love, living a dream I had for so long.
If you were love's promise, then I would be time,
your constant companion till stars align.
And though we are mere mortals, true love is divine,
and my devotion eternal, to my one valentine.

KA. PARINASRI

KA. PARINASRI
From Chennai!
Writing is her passion!
She owns a writing page, where her pen bleeds more than her talks!
She is not much easy going, but yet she is kindhearted and friendly too!
She adores to help others, she tries her level best and supports in all her possible ways, when people are in need!

Emotions

The Most Hurtful Moment...
When you say you're coming!
I be waiting just for you here like a Mad!

And finally when I wanna bother what the hell is up with you?
You be like
'I can't come today'

My question is then why the hell?
You promised me that you'll be coming for sure?
Giving me a hope, and then pushing me into a hurtful situation?

Darling understand you may occur simply or maybe just for namesake.

But I blindly believe in you, so each word which you occur hits my heart!
So please from next time keep up on your words and promises!
Instead of cheating and hurting!!

Sometimes whatever you do just hurts me so badly! But I had never told about it to you!
Instead I bidder it within me, and let the emotions in the name of tears rolling down my cheeks!
Never knew why I love you blindly!!

Falguni Mundhra

This is Falguni Mundhra from Odisha. Being a girl, she has faced all the common as well as extra problems a girl faces.

May be humans are not trustworthy in this world, but for her books are always.

She really loves reading novels. Indian epics are always her favourite and among them Mahabharata is one of her favourites.

She believes writing is the best medication to all her problems.

MAY BE MY LOVE STORY

Being calm as the moon
I looked at the world
Found only you
To be my moonlight

From the first sight
You became my deep sea
My waves may go
To fascinating shores
But the regression will always be
To your tender deep-ness

You may call me your daffodil
Wordsworth won't steal me
But those jovial moments of us
Will always be William's daffodils

I stare at you,
Because my world was there
I see a Paris in you
You see a Helen in me
My love, we are ready
For another Trojan tragedy!

-Falguni Mundhra

Shefali

Shefali is a budding poet, begun her journey of writing poems while she was 8, and resumed it again after 8 years. She mostly writes of melancholy and love.

LOVE

I look into your eyes,
What a beautiful sight,
I feel like I could touch the skies,
Even at my lowest, I gather
all my might.
The heart you own,
Is made of gold,
As I have known,
The part of you that I did unfold.
You taught me that love
will perish,
If we compare,
The bond that we cherish,
And the love that we share.
Love is fascinating,
It's a feeling very rare,
It will happen to everyone waiting,
Still unknown when and where.
It happened to you and me,
When the Cupid played its game,
You and me became we,
And closer we came.

Yamini Sona Vaishnavi

Yamini sona vaishnavi is a budding writer who pursues her III UG of English Literature in Madurai, Tamil Nadu. She has a great love for playing with words and passion for reading and writing, especially poetry and quote writing. She is currently co-author for so many anthologies and wishes to write more. She started writing from her school days, where she used to contribute for yearly magazine and continued the same in her college too. She wishes to touch the hearts of the readers through her poetry.

Purity's at its peak:

A month of surprises, chocolates, flowers and greetings!
A month of proposals and confessions of souls!
A month of plans, love letters and praise!
How can I explain this period of elegance!
where souls of charm, combine together!
Cuteness gets overloaded when that concealed fear comes out,
making them finally tell their love to their soulmates after,
waiting for almost, days, months and years together!
Some telling the words "I love you!" Some, "I need you!"
Some, "I want you!", Some, "We are meant for each other!"
I am able to hear these lovely words, from both the gender!
For, they live lives with one soul and two bodies!
They feel this fact that, they are flying with each other!
More than living their lives for themselves, these definitions
of purity,
Live a life, everyone looks and yearns for!

Sourabh Bhakar

Sourabh Bhakar, often called imaginative writer is a 17 years old young writer from Sikar, Rajasthan. Currently he has been doing schooling. He has the desire to change this world by making people understand true meaning of life and the way he found to do this is through his writing.

Blurred Love of Valentine

Since a very long time I have been waiting for you,
All time I find new ways to meet you.
then happens something miraculous
in the month of love - February!
and two souls meet,
like sugar in jaggery!
Now you are like sunshine in severe cold,
which makes me more bold.
you are like veins of my heart,
which offers more comfort.
you are like light of my eyes,
which the world more bright.
You came on my life on valentine's day
and now my every day is valentine's day
Let's show this opposing world,
This soul separate never,
our unending love is forever....

Love forever

Before few years, we meet on this special day,
And before few time we separated on a scary day.
Wish you could be here today with me,
like this heartbeat.
then I would not be alone,
like this deserted street.
At night, I often find myself,
looking up and finding you in stars
maybe you're that bright one.
At morning, I try to find you with first sunrays.
Every time I feel you are here,
moving with blowing wind.
which squeezes me too see behind.
And i saw blurred past instantly
me and you hugging very secretly.
but this mysterious world is too clever
which don't like us together
But wherever you are don't forget
we are together forever
and our love is forever.

NESBA SAHIR

She is NESBA SAHIR, daughter of MR. SAHIR KHAN and MRS. BEENA SAHIR. She is from kollam,Kerala .She is an aspiring electronics and communication engineer. She turned her can'ts into cans and her dreams into reality. She is a creative writer as well as motivational quotesmither. Her first love is writing. She is not a professional writer but she is very passionate about writing and love to pen down whatever comes in her heart. She likes to travel a lot as well as likes to meet new people's. You can contact her via with mail: nesbasahir68@gmail.com Instagram id: nesba_sahir

Valentine Day!

I love you more
than you love me!
I care you more
than you care me!
I hate you more
than you hate me!
I protect you more
than you protect me!
I respect you more
than you respect me!
I concern you more
than you concern me!
I value you more
than you value me!
I know you more
than you know me!
I need you I love you.
I am for you, babe.

Ms. Ishrat Jahan Noormohammed Khan

Ms Ishrat jahan khan is a passionate Teacher and a Writer she loves reading and writing. Loving and caring is her hobby. And keep learning and accept the positive suggestion is her quality.

She belongs to North India and stays at Ulhasnagar (Maharashtra).

Loves humanity always.

Love month

Yes, love month
Is the blessed month
And February is that month
Which care for faith

It ignores hate
It is never late
It captures fate
It makes your state

Love grows in positive
It destroys the negative
It makes you active
It helps you when you are possessive

Makes the things pure
And care for true
It need a dare
So that your love can care

Be always happy
Don't be Stacy
It's a month of love
Your love symbol is dove...

Jeevitha. S

She is a girl with stupendous writing skills. Her heart is a castle abound with unbreakable courage, being contained with enticing dreams. Penning is her way of spreading aesthetic vibes among her readers. Being a literarian is her pride. She loves to be a unicorn amidst the flock of sheep's!

Exceptional feeling of love!

Warm wind and freezing breeze felt together is that possible, someone asked ...?

I replied back by saying that, yes... it is possible and I also stated to them that "believe me I have experienced it rather".

How come, it's impossible! they replied.

Yes, it is possible...!

It happened to me, when my love held my hands and kissed me on my forehead;

I felt both warmness and coldness together!

HEMA KIRTHIGA J

She is Hema Kirthiga J, and her pen name is sparkle. She is professionally a psychologist and passionately a writer. She heals others but writing heals her. She is writer, reader, orator and a believer. She is from Chennai. She lives by the principal of inspire and be inspired. She writes her heart and soul and she deeply believes that the depth of her heart and the nib of her pen are soulfully connected. Writing is an art and she is a proud artist. She loves what she does and loves what she writes. You can reach her at

Instagram- @the_pen_queen
Email- inker.sparkle@gmail.com
Yourquote – JKM

DAYS OF LOVE!

Hey February,
You know,
You are my favourite month,
Though you are short,
You fill my heart to brim,
Though you are could,
You warm my heart,
Your days are filled with love,
Your days are filled with care,
You make couples happy,
You remove their pain,
You break all the fights,
You remove all the misunderstanding,
Though you don't care,
You bring smile in many,
You become favourite in various,
You remain the beautiful memories,
In many love story,
You uphold the enthusiasm,
You break the surprises.

Adarsh Kumar Pandey

Adarsh Kumar Pandey popularly known as Prince, started writing when he was just 14 years old.

He is passionate to become a successful writer as well as he wants himself as computer Engineer.

Looking on the situation of unemployment in India, he decided to help the Indian government and unemployed and decided to become a successful computer Engineer.

February The Month of love

Again it's February of love
The February short in terms and relation
The February of entering into huge innovation
The February of engaging with one another
The February of capturing the love together
The February seeds up the love in short
The February breaks heart' allot
The February a season of bond
The February keeps everyone beyond
The February of breaking concession
The February of thoughtful communication
The February of retiring emotions
The February end with love promotions.

You & Me

I'm still awaking
Because I haven't slept
I'm STUPID
Because i haven't loose
I'm wandering
Because i haven't get
I'm searching
Because i haven't found
I'm the one
Because i haven't seen.

 You are the runner
 Because i haven't run
 You are winning
Because i haven't start
You are barking
Because i haven't roar
You are laughing
Because i haven't smiled
You are Rubbish
Because you haven't know me

Kruthigayini K G

A budding poet. She writes in both English and Tamil. You can take a look at her writings in Instagram @_out_of_box__

The Magical Bond!!!

The moment.,
Art of love...
Became Part of Hearts...

She Became the Music...
To his Lyrics!!!

He Offered the Island...
In her Oasis!!!

She Nurtured the Nestle.....
Merging with his Valiance!!!

He Derived the Doodle...
Eliciting her Energies!!!

No matter...
Changes in the MIND,
Due to the different TIME,
The BOND that remains same,
ever hidden is LOVE!!!

S. Subhashini

Insta ID: @subhashini_srinivaasan

An Aspiring writer as well as student trying to inspire heart through her words. She has magic in her words. It goes into everyone's heart and enrich the soul. She sees love in everyone with her words. She attracts everyone to her side with love.

"true love never fails in this world, so spread love and positivity."
According to her.

Speciality of Love

Love is like a wind
Only we can feel it,
It has no image
But it is everywhere...

No one knows,
Where it will come from
And when it will go
It's like a thief...

The same is true in love
Comes like a thief
It steels our heart
Without knowing us...

It connects two hearts together
It joins with two loving souls,
Turns the two together
This is the speciality of love...

Samia Riaz

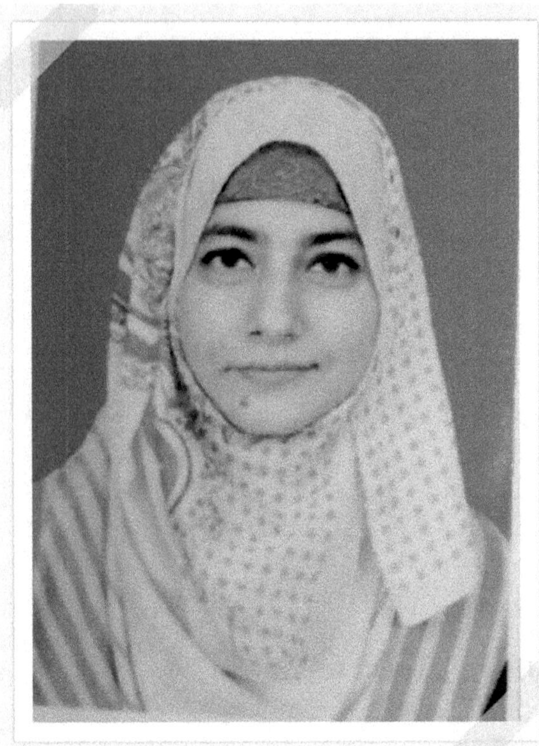

Miss Riaz has done her graduation in Inorganic and Analytical Chemistry. She's an educator by profession but has been working as a freelance content writer for more than 3 years now. She has written articles for quite some online firms and have been highly praised for her work.

Love - the Essential Aroma for Merry Life.

To whatever religion you belong, the Divine Scriptures tell you how love was the basis of the formation of this universe.

From the love of God for its Creation, the love of mountains for flowers, the love of parents for children, the love of lover for his/her partner, the love of food for a foodie, the love of an influencer for fans, the love of worldly goods for a miser and whatnot, love is the reason to all cycles going on. Johnny Lennon rightly wrote, " all you need is love."

It takes a second to hurt someone, so does it take to create a loving concussion. Such hearts, that honor you, are priceless! Cherish these hearts. Pay attention to what they say - it comes straight from the gut and soul.

as it dawns with this sun breath-taking
a new day arrives with new undertakings
there is hustle and bustle everywhere
with people trotting to wrap their takings

alongside burdens runs the emotion of love
that binds all the creatures even in strife
for God or you, myself or a dear wife
love is the essential aroma for the merry life

Manmita Sarmah

She hails from Assam. Her hobbies include reading, watching movies, listening music. She occasionally writes poetry. She is currently pursuing her PhD in American Literature from Gauhati University.

Autumn Love

Again came the autumn,
With its crisp and mellowed halo!
Bringing forth the
Fond memories of last winter.
When I snuggled by the fireside,
Holding your hand, ruminating
The bygone years!

Three years have gone by,
Watching yellow leaves fall,
Weaving a carpet
Of bittersweet moments,
Caressing the grass beneath!

Tea in our hands,
As refreshing as October breeze,
And we watched the moon!
Dripping by the river,
Making a canvas of its own.

Love found its way
Through creeks and crannies.
Only to be rejuvenated
By the autumnal mist!
And never to be frazzled by the
Occasional showers of monsoon!!

Ankita Sahoo

Hello everyone she is Ankita Sahoo. She is currently doing her graduation in political science. She is an introvert and a bookworm by nature. She is a writer as well who is extremely passionate about penning her thoughts. She wants to be an IAS officer with a purpose to serve the nation.

LOVE OF MY LIFE

You are special to me as a rose is, among all other flowers.
The warmth of your touch, makes me crunch.
The way you smile, makes me smile.
The way you look deep into my eyes, as if thousands of
words are exchanged just in a glance.
And it makes me feel your love just at once.
You didn't give me any bucket of flowers,
Nor did I expect any expensive gift showers.
Neither you need to rent the moon,
Nor to bring me chocolates and balloons.
I just need you and your precious time,
Your love, care and respect for lifetime.
We may not meet in the month of love,
That will not mean the end of love.
We may not go for romantic dates at night,
Still you are my Mr. Right; for whom I will always fight.
No matter where you are and where am I,
But our love will always be on our side,
I wish you all the happiness of life.
May you fly, above the sky.
May you get a healthy, wealthy and desired life,
As you are my saviour for the rest of life.

Suryakanta biswal

He is suryakanta biswal of class 11th of puri the icon city. He wishes to be a writter in passion and chhated accountant in profession

LOVELY VALENTINE

Before I was a lover
always boarding in my own shelter
 thought love would never stop by ever because I couldn't
find that special lover
then I meet you in one winter
for hours we talk to each other
 As stranger we are
We don't know about each other
 I fill then I have found the perfect partner
Someone I could love forever
Every day with you gives a thrill
All my dreams you reachly fulfill
Your eyes tell me that
You will love me every day
Now my love grows deeper and deeper
And life with you becomes sweeter
At last the day comes
When I say goodbye
Promise me you won't cry
Because the day I will be saying
That will be the day I die

Monika Shanmugam

Monika Shanmugam is a 22-year-old writer, poet and essayist, professionally pursuing her career as a homoeopathic doctor in Tamilnadu. She is a co-author of many e-books and anthologies. Nature and the universe inspires her to pen down her poetries. Besides, she writes on the subjects of emotions, love and motivational messages.

YOUR SKIN TASTES LIKE!

Your skin tastes like my midnight chocolate cookies
That I crunch to quench the acidity of my insecurities.
I touch your skin but you pinch my touchy heart,
Which for many years abided your love knot.
The touch of your skin reminds me the warm solace
Of my midnight lover, the moon which vows me always,
That I'll get someone better than him
And I'll love someone more than him.
I'm baffled, how should I feel now?
Either ecstatic for the triumph of getting your love,
Or low for losing to the vows of the moon?
You, my bloke, Give your answers soon.
Before the dawn comes, with your brutal hugs and smooches.

Vaibhav Gupta

This is Vaibhav Gupta belonging to Kanpur, UP. He is a graduate and had working in hospitality department. He has keen interest in poetries and stories. He has recently authored the e-novel "it happened in delhi" and is working on few more. Besides, He has been actively participating on events those lead him to his passion. His works can be witnessed by his insta id- @thevaibhav_gupta

Love street

I still remember our first meet,
With the morning breeze,
In near to your home street.

The joy of our meeting you,
Clearly visible was on my face.
Spending moments with you,
Made me feel so amaze.

It was just a morning of February,
My lips want to taste your lips,
Like it's my Cadbury.

Holding your hand felt like heaven,
I swear honey trust me,
Your beautiful eyes are weapon.

With you I want to spend my rest of life,
I want you to become my Wife.
Our kids will play in those streets of our town,
I want you to say that I'm your more than I'm ow

Flairs and Glairs, a platform by a student for the students. We are esteemed youth struggling to carve out our path for our future and we follow a basic mindset Since everyone is not born with all-round skills. Joining hands with people who are born to execute it with perfection is the best way to evolve. Self-Evolution is the need of the hour but, evolving as a community is what we strive for. The initiative as kickstarted by, Founder- Mr. Shubham Shah with the motive to utilize the skillset and talent of writing has now a team of 10+ people who are actively participating into newer forms of learning and discovering talents among youngsters. We Provide platform and services like Publishing opportunities, Open mics, Workshops, Hands-on training. Operating with Brand Name of Flairs and Glairs (Publication House), we offer the chance of elevating a passionate writer to an esteemed author With Brand name Teekhe Zasbaaat. We bring to you an opportunity to get accustomed with the Public Speaking and Presenting of Thoughts along with regular challenges to brush up your inking spirit. The newest initiative to extend our services we introduced in a new writing Platform- The Glittering Fables and Ink Over Tears.

We Choose to Fly Like A Falcon than to be

a Leg Pulling Crab.

To Know More: Infoline – 7781900870
Mail Us At-
flairsandglairs@gmail.com / info@flairsandglairs.in
Or Visit is at
www.flairsandglairs.com / www.flairsandglairs.in
Social Handles- @flairsandglairs @teekhezasbaaat

9 789390 799732